A simple, unpredictable text, zany diagrams and offbeat illustrations combine to create a hilarious twist to the age old question: *where do babies come from*?

"Cole's drawings and simple text are candid without being offensive and, without getting terribly complicated or serious, communicate the essentials of conception and childbirth in a direct but light-hearted manner that will leave everyone grinning and no one embarrassed."
—*Publisher's Weekly*, starred review

"The full facts about human reproduction, ingeniously set in a story . . . a notably fresh, matter-of-fact approach."
—*Kirkus Reviews*

". . . an accessible, humorous, accurate look at where babies come from."
—*Booklist*

Winner of LA Parent Magazine Book Award

To Tom, Sarah,
Nigel, Sabrina and Kim
for their kind help
and advice

Mommy Laid an Egg!

or Where *Do* Babies Come From?
by Babette Cole

chronicle books

"Well," said mom and dad.
"We think it's time we
told you...

"...how babies are made!"

"OK," we said.

"Girl babies are made from sugar and spice
and everything nice," said mom.

"Boy babies are made from slugs and snails
and puppy dogs' tails!"
said dad.

"Some babies are delivered by dinosaurs."

"You can make them out of gingerbread!" said mom.

"Sometimes, you just find them under stones," said dad.

"You can grow them

om seeds," said mom.

"Or just squeeze them out of tubes!"

"Mommy laid an egg," said dad.

"It exploded!

And you shot out!"

"Hee hee hee, ha ha ha, hoo hoo hoo, what a bunch of nonsense!" we laughed.
"But you were right about the SEEDS, the TUBE, and the EGG!"

"We'll teach you how babies
are really made."

"Mommies do have eggs. They are inside their bodies."

"And daddies have seeds in seed pods outside their bodies."

This fit s

"Daddies also have a tube.
The seeds come out of
the pods and through the tube."

in here

"The tube goes into the
mommy's body through
a hole. Then the seeds
swim inside using their tails!"

"Here are some ways...

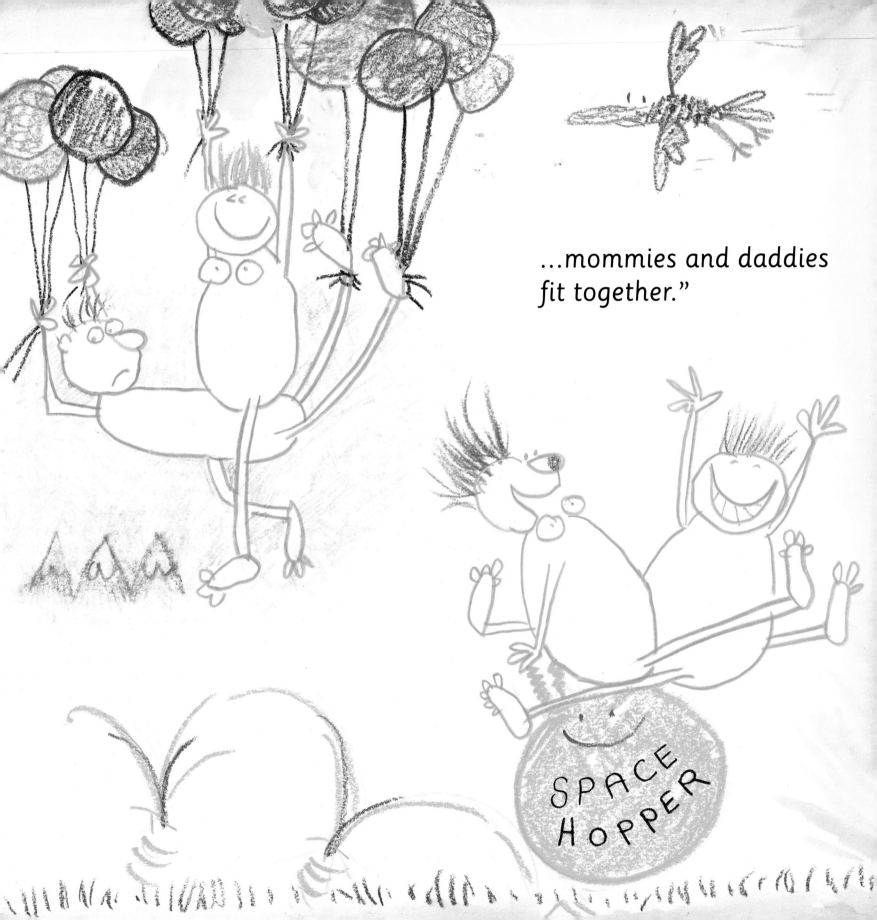

...mommies and daddies fit together."

SPACE HOPPER

"The Baby gets bigger...

"The Mommy gets fatter...

"So now YOU know...

...and so does everyone else!"

First published in the United States in 1993 by Chronicle Books.
First published in Great Britain in 1993 by Jonathan Cape Ltd.

Text and illustrations copyright © 1993 by Babette Cole.

Library of Congress Cataloging-in-Publication Data
Cole, Babette.
Mommy laid an egg! / by Babette Cole.
p.   cm.
Summary: Two children explain to their parents, using their own
drawings, where babies come from.
ISBN 0-8118-0350-3 (hardcover)
ISBN 0-8118-1319-3 (paperback)
1. Sex instruction for children--Juvenile literature. [1. Sex
instruction for children. 2. Reproduction.] I. Title.
HQ53.C64 1993
649'.657--cc20   92-38306
                                                  CIP
                                                  AC

ISBN 0-8118-1319-3

Manufactured in Singapore.

10 9

Chronicle Books LLC
85 Second Street
San Francisco, California 94105

www.chroniclekids.com

Babette Cole has written and illustrated many books for children, including *Babette Cole's Beastly Birthday Book*, *The Hairy Book, The Silly Book*, and *Princess Smartypants*. She also works as a printmaker and designer. A graduate of the Canterbury College of Art in Kent, England, Ms. Cole now lives in an old cottage in the English country-side with her beloved dogs and horses.